Dedicated to Manny, Leah, Joe and Moe

A whimsical tale of fun, fantasy and
frivolity about...
The best game ever played;
The best sport ever made;
Down which nostalgic memories cascade.

Acknowledgements

The following is a list of persons to whom I owe a debt of gratitude for having transformed this fantasy into a reality, and who have been instrumental in lending, and have inspired me to lend, my penmanship and creative imagination to paper and dissemination.

Manny and Leah; Protagonists I couldn't have done without. Their passion for, and deep appreciation of, the Game, is laudable and infectious.

Mary Jo Stresky, of The Write MoJo Literary Services – the greatest editor west of the Mississippi.

And last but not at all least, my good friend and confidant, Mr. Morris Heber – a true friend like no other.

DREAMS OF FIELDS
A Cooperstown Tale

A Novella
By
Stephen Hunter

Tiny rabbit claw and squirrel paw prints were the only things disturbing the otherwise pristine snow spanning the entire park abutting the back yard.

Bent naked pine, dogwood, aspen, sycamore and balsam fir branches had nearly buckled under the weight of the white powder that hadn't made its way to the ground.

And though birds were chirping and Punxsutawney Phil may not have seen his shadow, the bitter winter that had temperatures and snowfall not seen since the Flying Dutchman's masterful 1908 season didn't appear to be abating any time soon.

"It's here! It's here!" Dad shouted enthusiastically into the kitchen.

"What's here?" Leah inquired turning away from the window.

"Remember? The idea we proposed? I got the email, see?" Dad said, as he unfolded a white sheet of paper and handed it to her.

"They like it, and they're considering it for 2017. In the meantime, they sent us free VIP passes and three nights' hotel stay for the big 75th anniversary next summer! Wow! Now it's my *dream's* turn."

"We gonna go?" asked Leah.

"Of course we're going. It's going to be an anniversary celebration we can't miss."

"Dad, what does VIP mean?" Leah asked.

"Very Important Persons. It entitles us to better seats at the festivities, and we get to access the Archive Section. Few people get that privilege."

"Cool. But Dad," 11-year-old Manny broke in, clutching something in his hand. "I can't stand winter; when's summer gonna be here already?"

"Well," Dad answered, "winter is long, especially this year. But we can reminisce of summers past, and look forward to an exciting fun-filled coming one. That should ease Jack Frost's pinch."

"Who's Jack Frost?"

"Jack Frost's a nickname given to bitter winters, like this one.

"Manny, you know who Rogers Hornsby was?"

"I think so. He played for the Cardinals and Cubs. He often switched between three positions -- second, third and shortstop."

"I'm impressed you know that. But do you know what he said?"

"I guess he said many things."

"Yes. But one that's specific to right now. He said: *People ask me what I do in winter when there's no baseball. I'll tell you what I do. I stare out the window and wait for spring.* Do you think this is what he meant?"

Manny smiled at Dad agreeably.

Still staring out at the brilliant white abyss while tossing her favorite Georgia Peach baseball into the air, Leah chimed in.

"Dad, when did Hornsby die?"

"Why, I believe it was 1963."

"How old was he when he died?"

"Well, if he was born in 1896 he must have been 67."

"That's a short life, isn't it?"

"By today's standards I suppose it is."

"You're gonna live longer than that, right?"

"Well, I certainly hope so. But no one can ever be certain of that. We can all do things to keep ourselves healthier and live longer, like healthy diet and daily exercise, though there are no guarantees. Why do you ask?"

"Because I really like you, and don't want you to leave us."

Dad grabbed the baseball in midair. When Leah turned around he hugged her tightly, lovingly. Tears formed in both their eyes.

After a long minute Dad unlocked his embrace and asked, "Why all of a sudden, Leah? Why now?"

"Well, I think of the time we had this past summer in Cooperstown. I think about how short, fun and memorable it was. I didn't want that day to ever end. I want more of that, and I want it with you."

Dad smiled, still drying a tear of joy. "Summer was awesome. You're young yet, Leah, and there are many more precious moments and summers and winters to come chock full of fun and joy and wonder.

"Manny, what about you? What are you up to? Are you ready to return the Williams' card for safekeeping?"

"Yeah," Manny muttered as he took one last glance at the card and reluctantly handed it back to Dad.

"You know, Ta, tomorrow's another snow day," Leah continued. "Can you tell us a story, one of your 'summer tales' as you call them."

"Okay. Finish homework, eat dinner, and I'll meet you at eight o'clock, in pajamas, at the fireplace."

The three lay down side-by-side on the thick plush carpeting in front of the fireplace; Manny on the right of Dad, Leah to his left, and a cup of hot cocoa beside each.

Dad began:

* * * * *

The vivid white lane stripes whizzed underneath the late model Odyssey as it cruised down Highway 88. The air-conditioning was turned up full blast to tame the sweltering 85-degree temperatures during that late May afternoon. Manny and Leah could hardly contain their excitement, and found it difficult to sit still as the breathtaking countryside whipped by their window.

Though they had taken a similar trip a few years back to Canton, Ohio (home of the National Football Hall of Fame), this one promised to be more exciting, because the sport Cooperstown housed was far more intriguing to the three of them than was the one Canton did.

Though the plan was to visit all four halls of fame, Toronto and Springfield would have to wait, because now was Cooperstime.

Cooperstown! The name itself evoked great tales of awesome nostalgia, and raised goose bumps on their arms.

New York's Highway 88 was perfect. Magnificent rolling hills were on the left. On the right were valleys, meadows and creeks of clear, crisp water that created a landscape extremely pleasing to the eyes. The sun shone brightly, and visibility seemed as far as one hundred miles. The great American freeway was truly free and enchanting.

* * * * *

Dad would treat Manny and Leah to at least ten trips to the ballpark every season. He'd tell stories of earlier stadiums and their great legends, and assured them that the spirits of those legends still hovered there.

Baseball was in the Trio's veins. As soon as the Fall Classic drew to a close each year, they'd count the days -- sometimes the hours -- till Opening Day.

Though not a season ticket holder, Dad booked at least ten games well in advance of the home opener, and secured seating that gave Manny and Leah the all-around best possible baseball experience. Sometimes the seats offered a dynamic view. Other times, the seats were best to catch a homerun or foul fly ball. And at other times, the Dad selected the seats with the intent to give the kids the best possible experience from the most memorable sections in the ballpark, like Kaline's Corner or the Pepsi Rooftop.

Ballpark franks with mustard and sauerkraut, nachos, peanuts and bubbling Pepsi for the kids, and Labatt Blue for Dad, made Sunday afternoons unforgettable. A loss was okay, but nothing compared to a home-team win.

Evening duels were especially spectacular. Dad and kids would cherish the alluringly charming sight of the sun sinking behind the bleachers in right field, and the bright beaming ballpark lights incandescently bathing the entire stadium with a sense of summer-camp evening coziness. Then the downtown skyline's multi-colored lights would simulate an aurora borealis in the darkness surrounding the park.

On days that park attendance wasn't feasible, the three were soothed by the serenading play-by-play voice of the radio announcer and his sidekick color commentator.

On the no-school and no-camp days, the three walked to the park adjacent to their home. They'd bring snacks and drinks with them, and Dad would tune his Samsung Galaxy S4 to MLB At Bat Radio and listen to the game with great enjoyment.

The three would lie on the lush green grass and look up at the perfect July night sky. Besides for the radio announcer, the only other sounds were of Manny and Leah snacking hard on a fresh bag of Jalapeno chips, of straws sucking up the last bits of Slurpee, and the early evening chirping of thousands of crickets. Sometimes Mom would bake the freshest, juiciest apple pie for them to take with to their evening baseball picnics. That was truly the best of both worlds.

At the end of the 7th inning, Manny and Leah would head home and would be off to bed. They would slowly doze off to that remarkable baritone mellifluous play-by-play voice of their favorite announcer, Dan the Man.

Once they were fast asleep, Dad would quietly enter their room, kiss them on their forehead, and shut the radio off just as the post-game show was wrapping up.

Both Manny and Leah displayed wonderful dispositions. Manny was a fairly good athlete and loved playing all sports, especially football and soccer, though he loved following professional baseball. He did fairly well academically as well, and was a bright and enjoyable chap.

Leah was very sincere and studious, and was extremely gifted in softball and tennis. She was a natural at softball, and was her little league's captain for three consecutive seasons. She'd take home at least two trophies (that she proudly displayed in her bedroom) each season, for leading her league in several key individual baseball stats.

* * * * *

As they continued cruising down the highway, Dad shared with Manny and Leah the none-too-popular fact that only two men who had nothing to do with the sport of baseball are enshrined in The Hall. "Bud Abbott and Lou Costello" said Dad, "earned induction because of their very witty and celebrated comical baseball bit: *Who's on first?* "

When Manny and Leah said they too wished to be enshrined, Dad explained that it was unlikely, unless they too played the sport to unprecedented success. After all, only three hundred players (out of tens of thousands over the years) had been inducted since it opened its doors seventy-five years ago. But Dad further assured the kids that, like Abbott and Costello, there was another way in which to contribute to the sport that would be meaningful enough to earn induction.

When Manny and Leah insisted they would be enshrined, Dad chuckled and muttered to himself, somewhat audibly, **HOF**fentilch! (German for "hopefully").

* * * * *

Dad exited Highway 88 and continued onto Route 7. He meandered for about 25 miles through guardians of pine and sycamore that shaded the rural roads (making it seem as though they were travelling directly through the color green) while rays of sun splashed through the mighty tall brush, until they reached Route 20. The routes led them through some of the most dreamy-looking towns and countryside.

When they finally arrived at their destination, they saw a large sign that read, *Welcome to Cooperstown – Where it all began*. Beneath those words was a painted smiling baseball.

Instead of finding, as they were expecting, multi-million dollar contracts in place of asphalt, plush box suites to dot the archway, monolithic billion dollar stadiums to run as far and as deep as the eye could see, and billboards and marketing gimmicks displaying every kind of need and want, much to their delight, they found quite the opposite - Sheer beauty, tranquility and spectacular simplicity.

Dad, Manny and Leah observed children playing the sport they loved, and the one their quaint little village made famous. They watched them running and darting through cars along Main Street playing hide-and-go-seek or cops-and-robbers without a worry in the world, and without boasting that they were jumping and cavorting directly in the shadow of greatness -- in the shadow of "where it all began."

After a brief drive-by of Blackbird Bay at Lake Otsego, Dad steered the Odyssey down a road that slithered alongside the foothills of the Catskill Mountains, and finally arrived at the inn where they'd spend the night.

Driving the steep road down to the inn nestled in the valley below, the three observed a magnificent mountain range lurking behind the late afternoon haze.

* * * * *

Upon opening the Odyssey doors, the three were met by a wall of dead heat. As rays of sun pierced through the bulbous clouds, they breathed the musty summer air in and out in sheer ecstasy.

After checking in and unpacking, Manny, Dad and Leah enjoyed a quick dinner, and then made their way to the pool that they had all to themselves. Manny and Leah jumped and swam and played water ball with Dad.

The simplicity of this and so many other moments on this trip, reminded Dad of those summer weekend trips to Toronto with his dad to visit Grandma. And while there, the trips to Center Island, CN Tower and the Canadian National Exhibit.

These moments seemed to live in perpetuity, and put a smile on the faces of whom they touched. Dad hoped these trips with Manny and Leah would live in their hearts forever, and put a smile on their faces in twenty or thirty years.

Upon returning to their room, they grabbed a quick snack, watched some television and exhaustedly fell fast asleep.

Sweet *dreams.*

* * * * *

In spite of early morning news reports that a tiger was on the loose, the three were eager to begin their day of adventure. The most accurate suspicion was that the tiger had escaped from the nearby Utica Zoo, but nobody could offer a definitive confirmation. Though there were sightings, all witnesses could report was that while he appeared docile, the cat did have sharp claws, and that the tiger appeared to be as old as 30 (127 in human years).

The authorities weren't about to shut down the village for a day or two. Instead, police, paramedics, zookeepers, professional tiger trainers and sharpshooters were all summoned to sweep nearby forests, mountain ranges and even local streets to keep the visitors and residents safe from harm.

Though Manny and Leah were fearful, they were not about to allow fear to dash their *dreams*.

* * * * *

As Dad turned the Odyssey onto Main Street, it felt as though time had reverted back to the 1950s. It seemed as if all the cars, souvenir shops, benches and street lamp posts were from that fine American era. All this coupled with six blocks of baseball heaven.

It was ten o'clock by the time the three parked the Odyssey at Doubleday Field.

They finally arrived at a building that looked like an old schoolhouse. They stood motionless. Eyes affixed. Mesmerized.

The doors swung open, and inside, Manny, Leah and Dad were met with a life-size statue of two of the Game's greatest -- Ted Williams and Babe Ruth.

"Look, Leah! It's Ted Williams!" Manny shouted.

"*Sshh,* you need to keep your voice down in here," Dad warned.

"I know. But... but... it's him! It's really him!" Manny said more quietly, hardly able to contain himself.

"We know he's your favorite, but we have lots to see," Leah said, as she pulled her brother by his sleeve away from the exhibit.

* * * * *

On their way out of The Hall, Dad gave Manny and Leah each twenty-five dollars to spend at the souvenir shop. "Dad, can I get this?" or "Dad, can I get that?" the little voices would call out as Dad himself was examining some of the cute little knickknacks, mementos and objet d'art.

Dad paid the cashier, and the three made their way to the exit where they saw a large handwritten sign that read:

CAUTION: TIGER ON THE LOOSE!
Please inquire details and precautions to be taken,
at the Information Desk behind you.

* * * * *

It was now two o'clock in the afternoon. Four hours had flown by, though they all agreed they could have spent an entire day there, maybe more.

Dad, Manny and Leah strolled down Main Street and stopped to eat lunch at a picnic table in the tourist-teeming downtown. It was a fabulous day with bright sun and a light breeze.

As they were talking about their wonderful visit and experience, something suddenly caught the periphery of Leah's right eye. Startled, she quickly turned her head in that direction. When Dad and Manny inquired as to her sudden jolt, Leah realized it was a mere housecat -- not the cat that had been terrorizing the village. Leah and Manny breathed a sigh of relief.

"You know, Dad," Manny continued, "though they had nearly everything in there, I think they can use another exhibit Leah and I thought up."

"Interesting, explain."

"Well, you know for example the sign a manager may give his player to bunt? Or the sign either a base coach or manager gives his runner to steal? You know those weird hand gestures, like touching their caps, ears and nose?"

"Wow! Fascinating! You guys are good! Come to think of it, The Hall was missing an exhibit like that. I wonder why. Maybe you got something here. Leah, what do you think?"

"I think he's right, and I think we can add even more to that exhibit. For example, how about the signs an umpire makes when the pitcher pitches either a ball or a strike? And how about the different signs the umpire makes with his hands or arms on the third strike, depending on whether it's a swinging strikeout, tap foul strikeout or a looking strikeout?"

"And how about when the umpire double pumps his fist in a downward fashion when a player is caught stealing second? Or when he crosses both hands in open-palm fashion indicating safe on the same play?" Dad returned.

"Let's go back and propose it," Leah said.

On the way back to The Hall, Leah asked Dad, "Didn't you tell us earlier that Cabbott and Ostello got into The Hall without contributing to the game itself? And that only because of a comedy bit about baseball were they inducted?"

Dad chuckled heartily. "It's not Cabbott and Ostello; it's Abbott and Costello – that's first. Second, what are you getting at?"

"Well, you said we could also be in The Hall if we contributed in a 'meaningful way'. Wouldn't an exhibit like this qualify as a 'meaningful contribution'?"

"Ah! Whoa! I don't know! You may be onto something! If The Hall adds it as an exhibit, then I suppose so. Wouldn't that be cool?"

* * * * *

As the three finished lunch and headed back down Main Street, they noticed a bunch of idling police cars, ambulances and fire trucks. The village was abuzz. Dad and children felt very safe, though they were a bit jittery.

Dad approached the Information Desk at The Hall, and asked the attendant whether it was possible to speak to someone about their idea. The young woman escorted Dad, Manny and Leah into the office of Mr. Craig Leyland, Second Assistant Exhibits Curator.

He greeted the Trio kindly, then explained that he usually didn't take unannounced guests, but that when Kathy told him that a dad and his two children wanted to see him for a brief moment, he couldn't resist. "After all," said Leyland, "aren't dads and kids what baseball is all about? How are you folks doing?"

"We're good," Dad answered. "You've got a lovely museum. We're big baseball fans, so visiting this shrine is a *dream*-come-true."

"Great. Glad you enjoyed it."

"You guys have a lovely little hamlet here. We're not just in love with The Hall -- Cooperstown is amazing too."

"That's very kind of you to say. Yeah, we're certainly proud of this little town that brought all the big cities fame and fortune. So what brings you to my office?"

"My kids came up with a brilliant idea for an exhibit that seems to be lacking here at The Hall of Fame. So, how would we begin the process of submitting an idea or proposal?"

"That's a great question. When you get back home, send me an email explaining the exhibit." Leyland said as he handed Dad a business card. "I'll take it to the Board at their next meeting in September and we'll see what they say. However, I should tell you that we're pretty booked through 2017, with planning different exhibits and ideas. If the Board likes the idea, the odds of getting it installed into The Hall sometime in the future is pretty good."

"One last question," Dad asked. "If the Board decides to adopt our proposal as an exhibit, would Manny and Leah be inducted or enshrined?"

"Unfortunately, they wouldn't," Leyland said. Noticing disappointment in the children's eyes he quickly continued.

"But a bronze plaque with their names as contributors would be prominently displayed at the entrance to the exhibit. How's that?" Leyland said as he smiled at Manny and Leah.

Leah looked at Manny and smiled. Dad looked at both of them and also smiled. He then thanked Mr. Leyland.

As the three made their way out of The Hall, Mr. Leyland shouted, "Be careful out there. You know about the loose tiger -- his name's Raymond!"

Dad stopped dead in his tracks, and turned back to ask, "What did you say?"

"Nothing," Leyland retorted. "Just be careful. You do know about the tiger, right? This isn't the first time you're hearing of him?"

"Yes, we know about the loose tiger. But what did you say his name was?"

"Who's name?"

"The tiger's?"

"Oh, Raymond. Why?"

19

"No reason. It's just that I once knew a tiger named Raymond, and he was pretty darn fierce and frightening. For them to say he's no threat, or that he's old, or that his only weapon is his claws is simply untrue... if it's the Ray I'm thinking about."

"I don't know why you'd think it's the same one. All the more reason to be extra cautious," Leyland said, then made his way back to his office.

Manny and Leah were a bit more perplexed and fearful after that odd exchange.

"Dad, are you okay?" Leah asked.

"I'm fine; just fine."

"Why did you get so alarmed?"

"No reason. It's just that, well... it really doesn't matter," he said. "We've got a date at the wax museum, and it's getting late."

* * * * *

As the three made their way through the bustling crowd, they came upon a sign at 99 Main Street that read "Heroes of Baseball Wax Museum." They entered a dimly lit, musty smelling souvenir shop where the floor underneath their feet creaked with every step. Clothes racks and shelves were laden with sports paraphernalia and memorabilia.

20

"Excuse me, can I help you?" a voice asked from behind them.

"Certainly," Dad answered. "Are we in the right place? Is this the Heroes of Baseball Wax Museum?"

"Why, yes it is."

Dad purchased three tickets, and they were instructed to proceed to the rear of the shop where they'd find a door marked with the letters "W/M".

"For obvious reasons, everyone confuses that door for restrooms," the young ticket lady said. "But just enter there."

"What's back there?" Manny asked.

"You'll see," she said, as a mischievous look came into her eyes.

Leah asked, "Why is the entrance at the back of the shop? Why is it so dark and dingy? This is a bit too Twilight Zone for me."

Once they reached the door marked "W/M", Dad said, "Well, here we go. You guys said you wanted an adventure, so I guess we're about to have one."

The door creaked loudly as it was pulled open. One by one they entered. Slowly. Carefully. Methodically.

Leah exclaimed, "You've got to be kidding!" as Dad closed the door behind them after taking one last glance at the ticket lady smiling at him sheepishly from behind the counter.

* * * * *

Manny was all about sports trading cards. He had a large collection, some very valuable. The one card that always eluded him – the one he wished for more than any other -- was a Ted Williams autographed rookie card. He knew it was worth a mint, and the chances of obtaining one were rare. But he wasn't about to give up. He was adamant that he'd get lucky one day. He'd find one, trade one, locate one in one of those hobby packs he often purchased with extra money he'd earn at home doing chores or assisting neighbors with theirs.

If you asked him why Ted Williams, he wouldn't have a very clear answer. He wasn't a Red Sox fan, so it made little sense. But nonetheless he wasn't about to give up.

At first, Manny had his eye on the Honus Wagner 1909 T-206 card, but when Dad told him that one had just sold at auction for nearly three million dollars, he decided to set his sights on something a bit more within his range.

Dad had never disclosed to Manny that he actually owned a pretty special card: A mint condition, autographed, Hank Aaron rookie card, certified previously owned by the great Mickey Mantle. Dad was saving it for Manny for a very special occasion.

It was three o'clock.

* * * * *

A turnstile greeted the trio. They then entered a rickety old elevator, the door sliding shut behind them with a loud thump. Inside were two buttons: "START HERE FIRST" and "END HERE."

As soon as Manny pressed the "START HERE" button, the elevator lifted to the second floor. While it was creaking and groaning, Leah was thinking how it behaved more like the elevator in Roald Dahl's *Willy Wonka and the Chocolate Factory*.

The elevator stopped abruptly. The door opened.

Though it was dark, very faint sunlight made its way in through a window behind them, which covering was peeling. They felt their way until they came upon a black curtain.

Inside they were met by wonderful wax figures of Honus Wagner, Ty Cobb, Joe DiMaggio, Shoeless Joe, Ruth, Maris, Mantle, Munson, and Gehrig.

Turning a corner they found Manny's favorite -- *Number 9*, Ted Williams -- standing tall and proud with his million-dollar smile, bat in hand, and wearing the Beantown colors.

"Dad, it's him. It's really him!" Manny said, wishing he could reach out to touch him. "This is even better and more real than the one at The Hall!"

Manny asked Dad to take a photo of him with the *Splendid Splinter*. Dad obliged and took several of Manny and Leah with *The Kid*.

The three stood there cherishing the moment of being so close to one of the greatest hitters in all of baseball. Manny read the plaque about the life and times of Mr. Williams, as well as his record achievements, most notably his single season batting average in 1941 (.406), and career batting average of .344, both stats being in the all-time top ten.

Who knows? If not for his service in World War II for several years, there's a good chance he could have exceeded that batting average and other baseball statistics as well.

(Incidentally, the great Hank Greenberg of the Detroit Tigers volunteered for service at around the same time, which ultimately compromised his already impressive Hall of Fame numbers too.)

As the three were about to turn and move onto the next exhibit (one featuring the two alleged great inventors of The Game -- Doubleday and Cartwright), something caught Manny's eye.

"Dad!" Manny exclaimed.

"Yes, what is it?" Dad asked as he turned to Manny.

"Look!"

"Look where? Look at what?"

"There, in Ted's left hand. Don't you see it?"

Very dim lighting made it difficult to see anything but the figures' faces.

"I don't see anything."

"Look closer. He's holding something in his left hand."

Dad moved in for a closer look, while Leah already had and confirmed Manny's conviction.

"Kids, we can't touch anything here because this is a museum. We don't touch -- we merely look," Dad said. "I remember those instructions very well when twenty years ago I was visiting the famous

Louvre in Paris and I reached out to touch the Mona Lisa and was quickly reprimanded by one of the Museum's security staff."

"What's the Louvre? What's the Mona Lisa?" asked Leah.

"The Louvre's a world renowned museum, and the Mona Lisa is the most valuable piece of art in the world, painted by the great Italian born artist, Leonardo Da Vinci, about five hundred years ago."

Manny interrupted, not really interested right now in the history of the Louvre, the Mona Lisa or Da Vinci. "Can't we just sneak a peek at what he's holding?"

"I'm reluctant, but I suppose we can," Dad said, as he was as curious as the kids were about what Williams was holding in his hand. "If it doesn't budge, we're going to forget about it. Understood?"

Leah and Manny nodded.

Dad reached over the railing and snagged the card. It moved, but so did the wax figure.

Dad dropped his grip and froze. The children stood motionless.

"Hi, folks," came a voice from the figure as he dropped his bat and stuck his hand out for a friendly shake.

The kids and Dad were frightened.

"Ted!" Dad asked. "Is that really you?"

"Yes, it's really me."

"Holy cow! Kids, it's Ted!"

Dad shook Ted's hand, then turned to Manny and Leah and said, "It's okay. Go ahead and shake Mr. Williams' hand. This is a once-in-a-lifetime opportunity."

"But he's... he's..." Leah stammered.

"*Ssshhh.* Just go with it."

As Manny shook Mr. Williams' hand, he whispered, "Dad, it feels weird."

"It should. He's made of wax."

"Sorry folks, but I've got limited time as I must return to my post," Williams said. "But is there anything you'd like to ask me or tell me?"

"Mr. Williams, you're my all-time favorite," Manny said. "I noticed something in your hand, and I'm curious what it is."

Ted smiled and opened his hand to reveal a mint condition 1954 Wilson Franks HOF card, valued at about $20,000. Manny exclaimed, "Wow!"

"You like it?" Williams asked.

"Do I like it? My goodness! Wow! I love it! Can I have it?" Manny asked.

"You can if you promise to do something for me."

"Anything Mr. Williams! Anything at all! You're the best! What is it?"

"Promise me you'll follow your *dreams*. Whatever they may be and wherever they may take you. You'll be glad you did. Promise me you will."

"Yes, of course, Mr. Williams!"

"It may sound easy enough now," Williams continued, "but it isn't always. I want you to promise me that you will."

Eager to get his hands on this treasure, this heirloom, and to receive it from the legend himself, *The Thumper*, Manny nodded in agreement.

Williams bent down from his imposing 6'4" frame, handed the card to Manny and said, "You share that with your sister now, okay?"

Manny nodded excitedly while not taking his eyes off the gem he'd just been given by one of the most gifted players in all of baseball.

"One last question, Mr. Williams," Leah broke in. "You said you had limited time because you must return to your post. What post is that?"

Williams smiled proudly and said, "Why, Baseball Heaven of course. I want you kids to be your best in your summer softball leagues. I've been watching you, Leah, and you're the star of your team. Your average game is a single, double and triple with four RBIs. Even I didn't put up such impressive numbers.

"And Manny, you run like a cougar and your fielding is aMAYSing -- and I know aMAYSing when I see it. Why, I faced the great Willie MAYS many times in my career. Keep practicing and keep *dreams* alive. I promise it'll pay off in the end. Believe in miracles, and keep your heads high."

Dad, Manny and Leah were entranced and holding on to every word coming from Williams' mouth. They watched as he lifted his bat from the floor, tilted his cap toward his neighbors -- Doubleday and Cartwright -- with the hand in which he previously clutched the relic that was now in the hands of happy Manny. He then straightened his posture and froze into his former cryonic state, his eyes staring into the distance as if he had just hit a grand slam at Fenway Park.

The three stood affixed at the image, unsure of what just happened, but they knew it was special. They could hardly contain their excitement, and wanted to run outside and shout and recount to the world their big little episode.

After a long moment, the three backed away slowly and quietly. Not one word was said as each was wrapped in each's thoughts and wonderment. The silence in that musty, magical museum spoke louder than words ever could.

* * * * *

People were feverishly moving in all directions, and no one had time to stop and talk. Dad, Manny and Leah stared at this odd stirring of large crowds. The sidewalks and streets were teeming with many different folks, some in costumes. The clatter of marching bands could be heard off in the distance.

"Excuse me, sir. Can you tell me what's going on today?" Dad asked as he tapped one of the men rushing down the street slightly slower than the rest of the people.

"The Parade! Don't you know? The 7-Innings Parade!"

"The 7-Innings Parade?" Dad asked.

"Yes, the 7-Innings Parade. Once a year on the second to last Wednesday in May, we march up Main Street past the Hall of Fame and down to The Fields."

"The Fields?"

"Yes. *Dreams* Park."

"*Dreams* Park? Really? What then?"

"We all file into the stadium and enjoy the Game of Legends."

"Game of what?"

"Game of Legends."

"And what about the stray tiger?"

"Oh, yes," the fellow cackled. "Oh, yes. The stray tiger. Well, he ain't so stray after all."

"What do you mean?"

"Oh, you'll see."

"But it's pouring buckets of rain!"

"Did you say it's pouring or purring?" the man asked.

"Pouring, though I get the pun." Dad exclaimed.

"Yes. It is pouring, isn't it?"

The gentleman continued on his way while chuckling to himself and repeating out loud, "Oh, yes! Raining buckets. Raining cats and dogs. Oh, yes! Big cats."

Thinking the day couldn't get any stranger, an elderly grand marshal marched by twirling a baton. He tipped his top hat at them, motioned for them to join the parade, and kept on walking with the river of people.

Purchasing an umbrella at a nearby shop, Dad and the kids followed the floats, people in costumes, drummers, trumpeters and tuba players up the road to *Dreams* Park. In spite of the umbrella, they were soaking wet by the time they arrived, but they didn't care because it was the best day ever.

The parade disassembled and entered the park. Dad, Manny and Leah took their seats in the outfield, which were the only seats available by the time they got there.

The crowd seemed excited. They were laughing, talking, throwing baseballs into the air and catching them, and chowing down on some popcorn, corndogs, nachos, peanuts and Coca-Cola. But nothing was happening on the field.

A man, in his fifties, and seated near Dad, was pointing at the field while talking to a woman who appeared to be his wife. Unable to hear what the man was saying, Dad said, "Excuse me, sir?"

"Yes?"

"I'm wondering why everyone's here? Is something supposed to happen?"

"Why, of course."

"What? When?"

"The Game of Legends. Now."

"What is the Game of Legends?"

"It's your first time here, ain't it?"

"Yes, it is."

"Well then, you're in for a real surprise. I won't spoil the fun -- you just have to wait and see. You and your kids ought to be as good a crowd as you can be. After all, you know what the great Ty Cobb – star outfielder for the Detroit Tigers -- said? *'The crowd makes the ballgame'*."

"Cool! We're from Detroit!" Manny yelled.

"All the way from the Motor City, ay? That's pretty nice. Years ago your city was known as the Paris of the Midwest. Back in the day, Detroit was a more prominent city than even New York."

The man suddenly went silent and motioned to Dad and the kids to rise. A mass hush swept over the crowd, and they all rose to their feet. Late afternoon golden sunlight flooded the stadium just as a male voice broke the public announcing system:

"Welcome to *Dreams* Park at Cooperstown...where it all began. Ladies and gentlemen, please remove your hats for our national anthem.

"And now, ladies and gentlemen, the treat you've all been waiting for: The 2013 *Gaaaame* of Legends!"

The crowd applauded, whistled, thumped their feet and cheered.

"We will now introduce your teams and players.

"Batting first and playing first base for Team Hall, Ben Greenberg!"

Applause erupted once again as Ben made his way out onto the field lining up between home and third.

"Batting 2nd and playing right field, Louis Aaron!
Batting 3rd and playing 3rd, Harmon Clayton!
Batting 4th and playing left field, Sam Williams!

Batting 5th and playing shortstop, Lucius Benjamin!
Batting 6th and playing 2nd, Horn Rogers!
Batting 7th and playing centerfield, Joseph Maggi!
Batting 8th and playing DH is Ray Cobb!
Batting 9th and playing catcher is Peter Berra!
The pitcher for tonight's game is Sanford Braun.
Coaching Team Hall is Charles Dillon!"

After the team was lined up side-by-side, the crowd gave them a standing ovation.

"And now for Team Museum!

"Batting 1st and playing right field, Herm George!
Batting 2nd and playing 1st, Henry Louis!
Batting 3rd and playing left field, Joe Jefferson!
Batting 4th and playing 3rd, Edwin Lee!
Batting 5th and playing 2nd, Jack Roosevelt!
Batting 6th and playing shortstop, Peter Wagner!
Batting 7th and playing centerfield, Will Howard!
Batting 8th and playing DH, Mickey Charles!
Batting 9th and playing catcher, Gordon Stanley!
The pitcher for tonight's duel is Perry Johnson!
Coaching is George Anderson!"

Team Museum also received a standing ovation.

As the teams took turns at bat and on the field, Manny, Leah and Dad witnessed some of the greatest hitting and fielding. These guys were great on both sides of the ball, and seemed like something out of the building they had visited earlier.

It was the bottom of the ninth with one on and two outs, and Team Museum was leading by a score of eight to seven.

As Team Hall's designated hitter made his way from the on-deck circle, the stray tiger suddenly appeared at home plate. When the announcer cautioned the seven thousand spectators to remain still and not to panic, Manny said, "Easy for him to say. He's safe in the announcer's booth."

The tiger snarled and ground his frightening canines. Then while standing on his hind legs with bat in hand, Raymond the Tiger seemed to motion to the pitcher.

At the crack of the bat, the ball traveled all the way straight centerfield and landed in Leah's lap. While she jumped from joy, the stadium erupted into applause as Team Hall won the game nine to eight on Ray the Tiger's two-run walk-off homerun.

Leah was admiring her ball when she noticed an inscription that read:

To my best and most loyal fans: Leah, Manny, Dad.
Love,
Your friend and (Loose) Tiger
*Tyrus **Raymond** 'TY' Cobb*

* * * * *

At about five o'clock, the early morning light burst through the crack in the curtains of their hotel room. Tired from the previous day's long trip to Cooperstown, Dad, Manny and Leah ignored the sun's prodding and remained underneath their blankets in the arctic-tempered suite, and continued their cozy and satisfying slumber and *dreams*.

Three hours later they awoke. First Manny (he was always an early riser), then Dad, and finally Leah. They stretched, smiled to each other, exchanged niceties, and were eager to get out and start their day.

As Dad drew the curtains wide open, the full brunt of the sun made its way into the room, and the magnificent mountain range could be seen off in the distance. It was going to be a jam-packed day of fun and adventure.

As the Odyssey turned onto Main Street, the exhilaration in the air was palpable. It felt as if they had wound the clock back to the 1950s. It seemed as if all the cars, souvenir shops, benches and lamp posts were from that fine American era. And it was six blocks of baseball heaven.

Dad parked at Doubleday Field which was only a short distance from The Hall. The three felt funny, as if they had recently been here. In the words of Yogi Berra, star catcher for the New York Yankees, *it was deja vu all over again.*

Manny, Leah and Dad snuck a quick peek at Doubleday Field, then made their way along the old cobblestone streets dotted with plants, trees, lilacs, gardenias, sunflowers, tulips and other summery flora and fauna.

They finally arrived at a three-tiered, red brick building. Words on a sign on the building that were also etched in the cement below their feet welcomed them to the National Baseball Hall of Fame. The three stood there mesmerized.

When the doors swung open, Manny, Leah and Dad were met with a life-size statue of two of the Game's greatest -- Ted Williams and Babe Ruth.

A large semi-circular staircase carried them from the grand foyer up to the third floor where they were greeted by magnificent variations of former baseball stars' likenesses, photos and achievement awards. Showcases featured momentous baseball memorabilia such as bats, balls, hats, helmets, gloves and cleats.

Video screens throughout The Hall told amazing stories of the sport, and showed memorable times and triumphs in the game dating back to 1870. Some of the movies portrayed the changes in the rules of the game, and how baseball evolved from a farm-town sport to the most prominent prevalent sport of the 20th century, replacing horse racing as the sport of choice of the rich and famous.

Then as they descended to the next level, they were treated to a Women-in-Baseball-Exhibit, the Negro League exhibit, and an exhibit on the different styles and features of each of the thirty-two baseball teams and their parks.

There were also several rooms dedicated to several players who impacted the sport most. Hank Aaron, Babe Ruth, Ted Williams and Lou Gehrig were just a few who earned such special enshrinement.

Manny, Leah and Dad then made their way down to the ground floor where they found an exhibit featuring Hollywood's fascination with the sport captured in hundreds of films; the Scribes and Mikemen exhibit, displaying footage and photos of all those great journalists, announcers and play-by-play color commentators, like Harry Caray and Howard Cosell; as well as Inductee Row that celebrated the newest class of Hall-of-Famers.

But nothing compared to The Gallery that had nearly three hundred bronze busts, each with a plaque telling who each player was and what they did to earn induction. These were broken into classes by year since The Hall opened its doors in 1939, though the first class inducted was the 1936 one.

On the way out, Dad treated Manny and Leah to a few souvenirs at the gift shop.

* * * * *

The three had lunch at a picnic table in the town square. Catching himself daydreaming, Dad didn't realize that Manny and Leah had disappeared. He stood and looked up and down Main Street, then breathed a sigh of relief when he saw them speaking to an elderly man.

Though he had warned them never to speak to or follow strangers, this was no time for lectures. Thankfully the kids were fine and seemed to be enjoying their conversation. Dad wasn't terribly concerned, as he noticed the fellow Manny and Leah were talking with seemed to be about eighty years old, was well dressed and finely groomed. He didn't seem like your average stranger.

"Hello, sir," Dad interrupted.

"Hello, to you," the stranger responded.

"Where were you kids? I was worried sick!"

"But Dad," Leah spoke up, "we told you we were leaving for a minute, and you seemed okay with it."

"Okay? I don't recall you asking, and I certainly don't recall saying you could go."

"But Dad," Manny whispered, "you won't believe who this is."

"I don't care if it's Sandy Koufax himself, the greatest lefty who ever lived. It still wasn't a good idea to take off like that."

"But Dad," Manny continued, "it *is* Sandy Koufax!"

Dad took a few steps back and looked the man up and down. Coming in closer he noticed a familiar face.

"Sandy? *The* Sandy Koufax of the '55-'65 Dodgers?"

"It's me all right," Sandy returned, as he winked at Manny and Leah.

"But... but how did this happen? Why are you here? How did you kids know it was Sandy?"

"I can answer that," Sandy interjected. "I volunteer every year to manage the youth league at *Dreams* Park. As I was walking through town, I noticed your children staring at a poster featuring this five-day tournament. So I took the liberty to inquire about their love of baseball and their favorite team. And, well, here we are."

"Do you realize you're a living legend in our household?" Dad said.

"That's very humbling. I understand you're from Detroit, and that you're diehard Tigers fans."

"Yes, we are. Hey kids, did you know that Sandy is to-date the youngest player inducted into The Hall of Fame; he was only 37 years old?"

"You know," Sandy said, "I owe a great debt of gratitude to a truly great Tiger."

"Would that be first baseman, and fellow Hall of Famer, Hank Greenberg?"

"Yes, it would. He set the precedent, in an era when it was far more unacceptable, to refrain from playing on the holiest day of the Jewish calendar, Yom Kippur, for me to follow."

"We were happy to learn that Hank refused to play on Yom Kippur. And we were also very proud to learn of your great sacrifice to put God and your people before your passion and career," Dad said.

"Not to boast, but you do know that Mr. Greenberg's Yom Kippur absence was from a pennant race game, while mine was from a World Series game? I got a lot more flack for that, since we ended up losing that game against the Minnesota Twins."

"We're aware of that, which is why it's doubly impressive," Dad said.

"There have been some truly legendary players on the Tigers' roster throughout their one-hundred year history," Sandy said. "Even today you've got the best hitter in all of Major League Baseball, and arguably one of the best of all time."

"Indeed. Good ole' Miggy."

"I follow that guy every season, and would shudder if I had to stare him down from the pitcher's mound."

"He's our favorite," Leah said.

"As he should be," Sandy said, as he winked at her.

"Hey, I got something for you kids."

The kids watched Sandy remove something from his pocket.

"This is a mint condition Ted Williams 1954 Wilson Franks HOF card. Cards like these are rewarded each year to the best performers in various stats for the youth tournament I told you about. It was to be awarded to the winning pitcher. Unfortunately, we learned that one of the two pitchers is unable to make it. So the decision was made that I would serve as designated pitcher for both teams.

"The tournament's Board further decided that I would gift this card to any kid or kids of my choosing, who are in Cooperstown during my stay, and are within the league's age range of nine to twelve years old. Both of you qualify."

Manny, Leah and Dad could hardly contain their excitement.

Sandy noticed Manny trembling and tears forming in his eyes.

"Is everything all right?"

Manny nodded instead of speaking as he was so overcome with joy.

When Sandy handed the card to Manny, Dad asked Manny again if he was okay. Manny looked at Dad, then at Sandy, then back at Dad.

"Dad, you don't understand. I *dreamt* this last night."

"*Dreamt* what?"

"That I was given this mint condition Ted Williams 1954 Wilson Franks HOF card."

"You mean you *dreamt* that you met Sandy?"

"No. I don't remember exactly, but I remember this card in my *dream*. Wow! *Dreams* do come true! This is the greatest gift I've ever gotten. Thanks so much, Mr. Koufax. I'm honored and I love it!"

"Thank you," Sandy said. "But you must share with your sister. This is a very valuable card, so you'll want Dad to hold onto it for you."

Manny handed the card to Dad, but not before giving it to Leah to hold and observe for a moment.

"You two want me to toss a couple softball pitches to you?" Sandy asked.

"Would we!"

"Well then, what are we waiting for? Let's hop on over to Doubleday Field."

Manny grabbed his Cooperstown engraved bat he picked up as a souvenir, and marched up to home plate.

Sandy took the mound, and Leah and Dad were in the outfield. Manny took a few practice swings; tapped home plate several times with the barrel of his bat, then cocked the bat over his right shoulder. Sandy went into his wind-up and released the ball.

Strike One!... Strike two!... Strike three!

Manny tapped the fourth foul, and hit a soft blooper on the fifth right back to Sandy.

When Manny wacked the ninth pitch way behind Dad and Leah, Sandy smiled, applauded and shook Manny's hand.

Then Manny handed Sandy a black marker and asked him to autograph his bat. Sandy wrote:

To an awesome kid and wonderful hitter, Manny Hunter,
who swung at 10 balls pitched to him by Sandy Koufax,
and smacked one out of Doubleday Field.
Cooperstown, NY, May 22, 2013.

He then handed the bat back to Manny, and flicked Manny's baseball cap in acknowledgement of a job well done.

Now it was Leah's turn at bat. Her souvenir was a baseball glove, so Manny and Leah switched gear.

Leah swung vigorously at every Koufax pitch. She hit half of them -- two of which went deep into the outfield and one was a homerun. She was proud of her achievements, and Sandy made it known that he was proud of her too, by inscribing on her glove:

To a special girl and an even better hitter, Leah Hunter,
who makes Cabrera look like an amateur. She went 5/10
in a Koufax duel, something I did not come close to
achieving with the Dodgers in 11 seasons.
Doubleday Field, Cooperstown, NY, May 22, 2013.

Sandy Koufax

He then handed the glove back to Leah, and gave her a high-five in acknowledgement of a job well done.

Though Manny was a bit disappointed with his performance, Sandy assured him that though his hitting may not have been as good as his sister's, his fielding was far superior, and that he should take great pride in that too, because the old saying: *Defense wins games* is all too true. He encouraged Manny to keep on practicing.

Manny thought for a moment and then said, "Wow! That's what Ted Williams said to me."

"Who?" Sandy asked in astonishment.

"Ted Williams; Boston Red Sox' Ted Williams."

"Manny, you know that he's been dead twelve years? He passed before you were even born."

"Yes, I know. But I came the closest I ever will to Baseball Heaven last night, and it was magical."

"Hmmm. You've got a very healthy imagination, don't you?"

"Maybe. But this wasn't my imagination, and I remember everything that happened. Ted spoke to me and Leah at the Wax Museum."

"Good for you. I recall pitching to ole Ted, and it was no fun, he was just too good."

As they left Doubleday Field, Sandy wished them well on their journey. Dad, Manny and Leah shook his hand and thanked him, then went on their way wearing big smiles and a warm fuzzy feeling inside.

The three noticed some batting cages right outside Doubleday Field. The kids pleaded with Dad to allow them to do some batting practice. Dad responded that they just experienced the best possible batting practice they'll ever have. They persisted though and Dad relented.

Though neither did better than four out of ten, the attendant quoted the great Red Sox left fielder, Ted Williams: *Baseball is the only field of endeavor where a man can succeed three times out of ten and be considered a good performer.*

* * * * *

"Wow! I still can't believe we spent an hour with *the* Sandy Koufax," Leah said, as they continued back to town.

"He was really good at what he did, wasn't he," Manny said.

"He sure was," Dad said. "Like New York Yankees' star, Joe DiMaggio said, *'Pitchers are born pitchers'*. Sandy was a born pitcher. He was a pitcher's pitcher, and the best lefty.

"Why was I daydreaming earlier today?" Dad asked. "Why didn't I notice you guys walking away from lunch to meet Sandy?"

"How should we know?" Leah said. "Was it something about the Hall of Fame?"

Dad wasn't sure.

* * * * *

"Why is this wax figure missing?" Leah asked.

"That's strange. Did the sign say anything about why?" Dad returned the question.

"There's no sign either."

"No sign? A missing exhibit? Oh, yes. I got it. Follow me!"

Manny and Leah followed Dad out of the Heroes of Baseball Wax Museum. But as they were exiting the building, Manny asked Dad, "Why are we going? What happened? We want to continue."

"I know. Don't worry -- we'll be back. It's just that I now remember why I was daydreaming earlier. I have to do something first."

"Where are we going?" asked Manny.

"Back to the Hall of Fame."

"Why?"

"You'll see."

"Adults always say you'll see, you'll see," Manny said. "Why can't they just tell us what we'll see?"

* * * * *

When they arrived at The Hall, they stopped at the Information Desk. Dad asked the receptionist where the curator's office was.

"I'm not sure a curator is available. What's the matter? Can I help?"

"I have an idea for a new exhibit. I'd like to talk to someone about it."

50

"In that case, walk down that hallway to the last room on your right where you'll find a sign on the door that reads *Suggestions*. Inside are ballot-like sheets. Write your idea on one of them, and drop it into the Suggestion Box."

"I appreciate that, but what if I have questions? I'd like to know the general process and procedure."

"That *is* the process and procedure," the woman answered impatiently.

"No, I understand that part. But how will I know if The Hall accepted my exhibit idea? And does it entitle me to any recognition?"

"In that room you'll find a brochure you can take with you that describes the process. It should address all your questions and concerns."

"That's what I needed to know. Thanks for your help."

The room was spacious, and was stocked with plenty of scratch paper and pens. There was a water cooler, coffee and tea for visitors.

In plastic wall pockets they found pamphlets and brochures featuring different tourist attractions in the area, and a great deal of information on the Hall of Fame.

*IF YOU'RE READING THIS, THE LIKELIHOOD IS YOU
WILL NOT BE ENSHRINED INTO THE HALL.
HOWEVER, DON'T GIVE UP JUST YET, AS YOU STILL
HAVE THE CHANCE OF RECOGNITION OR EXHIBIT
NAMING RIGHTS...SO KEEP READING.*

So began the interior of the brochure entitled:

SOMETHING FOR EVERYONE...
...WITH AN IDEA.

Dad continued reading the brochure out loud.
Manny and Leah interrupted him; they wanted to
know what his idea was.

Dad explained that he wished to propose an
exhibit titled *Signs and Symbols of the Game.*

"For example, the sign a manager may give his
player to bunt? And you know the sign either a
base coach or manager gives his runner to steal
the base? Those weird hand gestures they make to
their players, touching their caps, ears and nose?
Or the signs an umpire makes when the pitcher
pitches either a ball or a strike?"

"How about the different signs the umpire makes
with his hands or arms on the third strike
depending on whether it's a swinging strikeout,
tap foul strikeout or a batter looking strikeout?"
Manny broke in.

"And when the umpire double pumps his fist in a downward fashion when a player is caught stealing second, or when he crosses both hands in open-palm fashion indicating safe on the same play?" Leah added.

"Yeah! Exactly," Dad acknowledged.

"Oh, this is so exciting! We may end up contributing to The Hall in a 'meaningful way' after all," Leah said as she high-fived Manny.

"Let's not get ahead of ourselves just yet," Dad said, as he continued reading the brochure. "What's this? 'Printed by the Leyland Group, Oneida County, NY.'? Oh, my goodness! It's all coming back to me. I *dreamt* last night that you two came up with this very idea for an exhibit, and that we came back here to discuss it with the curator –Craig Leyland.

Dad continued reading aloud:

Though there are no enshrinement rights to any non-member of Major League Baseball and or its affiliates, nonetheless one, whose idea for exhibit or artifact is included into The Hall, shall be awarded a special plaque at a ceremony which time and place shall be designated at the discretion of The Hall and its Board of Trustees, and shall be inducted into a special book known as the "Tome of Contributors", to be housed at all times at The Hall, in a showcase on the main floor of the Museum, directly across The Gallery of Inductees, in the Grand Foyer.

Furthermore, for a period of three years following the inclusion of such exhibit and or artifact, the contributor(s) name shall be prominently displayed on a plaque above the exhibit, along with the date of such submission, as well as the date on which such display was included and formally exhibited at The Hall. He or she shall also be included in the HCD (Hall's Computer Directory) by surname, which is located at the main entrance.

Finally, all such contributors shall enjoy lifetime complimentary membership to The Hall for s/he and immediate family members.

Dad pocketed the brochure. They left The Hall and returned to the Heroes of Baseball Wax Museum.

This too mimicked The *Dream*, only the legendary Tiger, Ty Cobb, was missing, just as Leah had reported earlier. Instead of finding him sliding into second base (or stealing home, which he did successfully 54 times in his career, and holds that record to date) with his right fist up in air, his sharp cleats pointing dangerously up at the baseman, and a ferocious glare in his eyes, the space was completely empty.

Leah noticed a makeshift sign in place of the usual description, which read:

Sorry for the brief interruption. The Tiger came loose early this morning, May 22, 2013, at approximately 3 a.m., though we are not entirely sure how or why. Ty is therefore out for repairs. We strive to give our guests the greatest and safest baseball experience. We expect Mr. Cobb to be out for no more than one week. We apologize for the brief inconvenience.

Leah smiled sheepishly; she knew exactly what this meant. She was perfectly okay with this minor inconvenience. Her *dream* too was about to manifest.

As the three continued looking around, a baseball suddenly fell to the floor, from where Cobb was previously ensconced. To make Cobb and his pose as real as possible, the Museum had hung a baseball from the ceiling just at the heel of Cobb, to demonstrate how his vicious screeching into second base many times caused the second baseman to drop the ball, ultimately rendering Cobb safe.

Leah picked it up and examined it carefully.

"What's that Leah?" Dad asked.

"I don't know; it just dropped right out of the sky. I think it came from the missing Cobb figure."

"Cool!" Manny said.

"I'm going to ask them downstairs if I can keep it," Leah added.

The manager examined the ball.

"Ah, yes, I know. This was with the Cobb figure. Yes, that wild loose Tiger is out for repair. Leave it to him and he'll claw his way out of a wax figure too. Where you guys from?"

"Detroit," Leah answered.

"Detroit? What a coincidence. Then you must be Tigers fans."

"We aren't just Tigers fans; we're *diehard* Tigers fans!" Manny said.

"Well then, it must be a sign," the manager said. "Little lady, you keep it and enjoy it."

"Is it a special baseball? Does it have any value?" she inquired.

"Other than sentimental, I don't believe so. It's just a prop we put up there on the Cobb figure. But sometimes what something means and the memories it brings is far more valuable than what it's worth in dollars," the manager said as he handed the ball to Leah. "You gotta love the Georgia Peach."

Dad and Leah thanked the man, and made their way out back onto Main Street.

As Dad watched Leah toss her ball into the air, and Manny hungrily looking at his Ted Williams card, he reached into his pocket and pulled out the brochure he picked up at The Hall.

He smiled and said, "Guys, the day is now truly complete. Our d*reams* have nearly all come true!"

* * * * *

Later over dinner, they talked about their experience.

"Kids, if there's one thing you take with you from this entire experience," Dad warned, "it's *classy sportsmanship*."

"What do you mean by that, Dad?" Manny asked.

"Well, the Great Mickey Mantle, star Yankee, said it best: '*After I hit a homerun I had a habit of running the bases with my head down. I figured the pitcher already felt bad enough without me showing him up rounding the bases.*' No matter what you do in life, no matter the sport you play, that's the kind of respect and dignity you should show others."

"Classy sportsmanship," Manny repeated softly as he stared at his Ted Williams card once again, unable to take his eyes off it.

After dinner they walked up Main Street for one last look at Cooperstown. Though they'd be leaving the little village behind, they'd be taking many wonderful memories and mementos they'd never forget or forsake.

As they approached the vehicle, Dad muttered, "Quite the odyssey."

"Yeah, it's a great car," Manny said, as he got into the back seat.

Looking back at Cooperstown, Dad said, "Whatever you say, Manny; whatever you say."

* * * * *

It was now six o'clock and they were exhausted. As they left Cooperstown, Dad looked in his rearview mirror to see the golden sun lick the tops of the buildings on Main Street, and repeated, "Quite the odyssey."

They eventually made it to back out to Highway 88 that took them to the 90 toward Buffalo and into Niagara Falls, Ontario, on route to Detroit.

After listening to music and talking about returning someday, grew thin, Dad scanned the radio and landed on a station that was broadcasting a Toronto Blue Jays game.

As they drove through London, Ontario, though, they could faintly make out the static broadcast of Dan "the man" Dickerson announcing a game between their Tigers and the Cleveland Indians.

What a way to end a trip of this caliber, thought Manny, Leah and Dad. It was as if the baseball gods were with them the entire way home.

As they crossed the Bluewater Bridge from Sarnia, Ontario, into Port Huron, Michigan, Dad looked into his rearview mirror to find Manny and Leah fast asleep.

It has to be more than coincidence, Dad thought, *that the Tigers game that night endured one of the longest rain delays in baseball history – two hours.* This delay caused the game to end almost perfectly timed with pulling into their driveway at one o'clock a.m., to an 11-7 Tigers' victory.

Dad woke the kids quietly, and Manny and Leah groggily made their way into the house, got into their half pajamas and snuggled into their pillows.

Wonderful waggish *dreams* and fantastic fantasies, of fairies that carried foul balls fair and fair balls foul, accompanied all three into deep slumber.

* * * * *

The following morning, the three awoke to a sumptuous breakfast Mom had prepared for the weary travelers.

Seeing how much love and tenderness she had put into preparing all the wonderful delicacies, Dad asked, "Manny, who did Lou Gehrig play for?"

"Why, the Yankees," Manny mumbled through a mouthful of toast. "I got a couple of his cards. Wanna see?"

"Maybe later," Dad said as he took Mom's hand. "It was the Great Gehrig though (who tragically died at the very young age of 37 from an awful disease now named after him) who said: *'When you have a wife who's been a tower of strength, a pillar of persistence, and has shown more courage than I knew existed – that's the finest I know.'*"

* * * * *

"Wow, Dad, that was terrific!" Manny concluded.

Leah agreed with a smile, as they lifted themselves off the carpet while embers smoldered and faded inside the fireplace.

It was eleven o'clock, and they were beat. They heard the cozy call of bed summoning them.

Manny and Leah followed the call, but not before thanking Dad for a wonderful whimsical tale of fun, fantasy and frivolity, about the best game ever played, the best sport ever made, down which nostalgic father-child memories truly do cascade.

THE TRUTH IS...

- Manny and Leah are real kids.

- The trip to Cooperstown actually took place as described in May, 2013 (except of course for all the fantasy).

- The Flying Dutchman is a nickname given to the great Hall of Famer, Honus Wagner of the Pittsburgh Pirates, who had a masterful 1908 season (and many more like it).

- The referenced winter was in fact the severest in both snowfall and temperatures in over 100 years.

- Rogers Hornsby, who was born in 1896 and died in 1963, is in fact another Hall of Famer, who played for the Cubs and Cardinals, and his quote is fact as well.

- Bud Abbott and Lou Costello were real as is their famous baseball comedy bit that in fact earned them induction into The Hall.

- Nearly all descriptions of people, places and events are true.

- Main Street, Blackbird Bay, Lake Otsego and the Catskills are all real.

i

- The general descriptions of The Hall of Fame and the Wax Museum exhibits, layout and setup are nearly all accurate.

- Ted Williams, Ty Cobb, Abner Doubleday and Alex Cartwright are in fact real people (now dead). Most of the facts, stories and quotes attributed to these individuals and others are accurate, as is Williams' career and single season batting averages.

- Ted Williams in fact is known by several nicknames, including "the Splendid Splinter", "the Kid", and "the Thumper".

- Dad visited the Louvre in Paris, and in fact nearly touched the Mona Lisa before being ridiculed by security.

- Hank Aaron, Babe Ruth, Ted Williams and Lou Gehrig enjoy extra special shrine treatment in the HOF for their phenomenal baseball accomplishments (as do several others).

- Harry Caray and Howard Cosell are in fact personalities as described.

- The exhibit idea is in fact real and was thought of by Dad, Manny and Leah during their trip to Cooperstown. The idea has in fact been proposed to The Hall and the

Board is considering it. It is also true that The Hall is booked with ideas and exhibits through 2017. (So if at all, this exhibit would be added after).

- Both Williams and Greenberg volunteered for WWII. This hiatus clearly cut into their already very impressive Hall of Fame numbers. Void of their service, they both could have very likely topped the list of many of Major League Baseball's key statistical figures. They both put country before self, and for that we salute and applaud them.

- A Honus Wagner 1909 T-206 baseball card recently sold for nearly $3,000,000.

- Detroit was in fact once upon a time known as the Paris of the Midwest, and was a more prestigious city than New York (primarily 1920s through 1950s).

- Sandy Koufax is real, and is still considered the best lefty that ever lived. He is still alive (and at age eighty looks younger than most sixty-year-olds). He holds the second all-time spot in career no-hitters (4), behind only Nolan Ryan (7). He was the youngest HOF inductee at age 37. He refused to pitch the first game of the World Series against the Minnesota Twins in 1965, in observance of Yom Kippur. The Dodgers lost that game, but ended up winning the Series in 7. Sandy lives in California and serves on the advisory board of the Los Angeles Dodgers. Detroit Tigers' Hall of Famer, Hank Greenberg's Yom Kippur's observance in the 1934 pennant race is also as described.

- Ty Cobb did in fact steal home 54 times, a record he holds to-date.

- Ty Cobb's nickname is the 'Georgia Peach.'

- The Tigers played the Indians that evening en route back to Detroit, (as did the Blue Jays), and the Tigers beat the Indians 11-7.

- Though the Game of Legends itself is fictitious, the players are not. In fact, they were all *from down the block*, and are all Hall of Famers.

Because the Book's plot calls for it, in the Game of Legends, I have either used the nicknames these players went by during their careers, and/or their second or less common names, in order to disguise their identities at the time.

Ben Greenberg: Hank Greenberg – Detroit Tigers
Louis Aaron: Hank Aaron – Milwaukee Brewers
Harmon Clayton: Harmon Killebrew – Minn. Twins
Sam Williams: Ted Williams – Boston Red Sox
Lucius Benjamin: Luke Appling – Chi. White Sox
Horn Rogers: Rogers Hornsby – St Louis Cardinals
Giuseppe Maggi: Joe DiMaggio – NY Yankees
Ray Cobb: Ty Cobb – Detroit Tigers
Peter Berra: Yogi Berra – NY Yankees
Sanfor Braun: Sandy Koufax – LA Dodgers
Charles Dillon: Casey Stengel – Brooklyn Dodgers
Herm George: Babe Ruth – NY Yankees
Henry Louis: Lou Gehrig – NY Yankees
Joe Jefferson: Shoeless Joe Jackson – Chi. WS
Edwin Lee: Eddie Mathews – Boston/Mil./Atl.
Jack Roosevelt: Jackie Robinson – Bklyn. Dodgers
Peter Wagner: Honus Wagner – Pitt. Pirates
Will Howard: Willie Mays – SF Giants
Mickey Charles: Mickey Mantle – NY Yankees
Gordon Stanley: Mickey Cochrane – Phila./Det.
George Anderson: Sparky Anderson – Phila.

Did you pick up on the subtleties?

1. Did you pick up on the *HOFentlich* reference?
2. Did you pick up on the aMAYSing pun?
3. How about Ted Williams' Cryonic State? Google it.
4. Tiger claws = Cobb cleats. Did you get that?
5. Did you noticed all *"dreams"* italicized?

www.ingramcontent.com/pod-product-compliance
Lightning Source LLC
Chambersburg PA
CBHW020318150626
46552CB00022B/2919